Dirty Bertie

PANTS!

For Lynsey and Paul ~ D R

For Philip, old friendships are the best ~ A M

STRIPES PUBLISHING
An imprint of Little Tiger Press
I The Coda Centre, 189 Munster Road,
London SW6 6AW

A paperback original
First published in Great Britain in 2007

Characters created by David Roberts
Text copyright © Alan MacDonald, 2007
Illustrations copyright © David Roberts, 2007

ISBN: 978-1-84715-017-2

A CIP catalogue record for this book is available from
the British Library.

Printed and bound in the UK

20 19 18 17 16 15 14 13

Dirty Bertie
PANTS!

DAVID ROBERTS WRITTEN BY ALAN MACDONALD

Stripes

Collect all the
Dirty Bertie books!

Contents

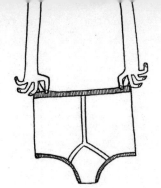

CHAPTER 1

It was Thursday morning at the swimming pool. Bertie was getting changed after the lesson with Miss Crawl. His clothes lay scattered on the cubicle floor.

"HA! HA! I CAN SEE YOUR PANTS!" jeered a loud voice.

Bertie snatched up his towel. "Who said that?"

"BERTIE'S WEARING BLUE ONES!" taunted the sing-song voice.

Bertie looked up. Two mocking eyes leered at him over the cubicle wall. It was his sworn enemy, Know-All Nick.

"Get lost!" said Bertie, throwing a sock at him.

Nick stuck out his tongue. "Make me, slowcoach!"

"Who are you calling a slowcoach?" Bertie demanded.

"You. You're always last to get changed," sneered Nick.

Bertie narrowed his eyes. "I bet I can get changed a lot quicker than you."

"Oh yeah?" said Nick.

"Yeah!" said Bertie.

"All right," said Nick. "Let's have a race."

Bertie could never resist a race,

especially if it meant a chance to beat
big-headed Nick.

"Suits me," he said. "Last one back on
the coach has to sit next to Miss Boot."

Nick considered it. A smile spread
slowly across his smug face.

"I've got a better idea," he said. "Last
one on the coach has to come to school
tomorrow in their pants."

Bertie's jaw dropped.

Dirty Bertie

"What's the matter, slowcoach, scared you're going to lose?" sneered Nick.

Bertie glared back. "Not a chance."

"OK, shake on it," said Nick. Bertie climbed on the bench and the two of them shook hands.

Bertie smiled. He would show that slimy slug who was slow. Nick wouldn't see him for dust. Wait till he told his friends about this: Know-All Nick coming to school in his pants – now that would be funny!

"Ready?" said Nick, through the wall. "Go!"

Bertie grabbed his trousers and yanked them on. His fingers wrestled with his shirt buttons. Socks next.

Dirty Bertie

Where was his other sock? He wasted precious seconds hunting around the floor on his hands and knees. Who needed two socks anyway? One was plenty. He jammed on his shoes, his jumper, his coat. He stuffed his soggy trunks and towel into his bag and burst out of the cubicle.

"ARGH!" Bertie tripped over a mop and bucket that someone had left outside the door.

Dirty Bertie

In seconds he was back on his feet and racing down the corridor. "Gangway!" he yelled, barging between Donna and Pamela. "Sorry! Emergency! Can't stop!"

Eugene flattened himself against the wall as Hurricane Bertie tore past. But turning the corner, a gigantic shadow fell across his path. "BERTIE!" thundered Miss Boot. "No running in the corridor!"

"But Miss, I—"

"Walk don't run, Bertie. WALK!"

Bertie groaned. He slowed to a walk as Miss Boot watched him like a hawk to the front door. Once outside, he flew down the steps, taking them three at a time. The coach was waiting in the car park. Almost there! Bertie dived through the door and flung himself into a seat.

"Yessss! I made it!" he panted. "I'm the

Dirty Bertie

first one back!"

"What took you so long, slowcoach?" drawled a jeering voice. Bertie gasped. No, it couldn't be! It wasn't possible! Know-All Nick lounged on the back seat. His hair was combed, his tie perfectly knotted and he wasn't the slightest bit out of breath.

"Tough luck, Bertie, you lose!" He smirked. "I am *so* looking forward to you coming to school tomorrow."

CHAPTER 2

Bertie sat in gloomy silence as the coach drove back to school. Darren pushed a bag of crisps under his nose. "Want one?"

Bertie shook his head.

"Are you ill?" asked Darren.

"Shhh!" said Bertie. "I'm trying to think."

"What about?" Darren munched his crisps noisily.

Dirty Bertie

Bertie sighed. "If I tell you, you've got to promise you won't breathe a word."

Darren leaned closer. "OK."

Bertie looked around to check that no one could hear. He dropped his voice to a whisper. "I bet Nick I could beat him back to the coach after swimming."

"And?" said Darren.

"And I lost the bet. Now I've got to come to school tomorrow in my pants."

Darren grinned with delight. "In your pants? HA HA HA!"

"Shut up!" hissed Bertie.

"No … but seriously…" giggled Darren, "…in your pants? Hee hee!"

"Keep your voice down!" pleaded Bertie.

"I can't help it. That's so funny," chortled Darren.

Dirty Bertie

Eugene turned round from the seat in front. "What's so funny?"

"Bertie's going to come to school in his pants," said Darren. "For a bet!"

Eugene stared at Bertie. "You're not?"

"No!" said Bertie, turning crimson. He was starting to wish he'd never mentioned it.

"But – in your pants?"

Dirty Bertie

"Stop saying it!" cried Bertie. "You're meant to be my friends. You're meant to help me!"

Darren crunched another crisp. "It's not *our* fault," he said. "You made the bet. What can we do?"

Bertie thought about it.

"I know," he said. "Do it with me!"

"What?" said Darren.

"Come to school in your pants," said Bertie, desperately. "We'll all do it, together. It'll be brilliant! Why don't we?"

Darren and Eugene stared at him.

"You've got to be kidding!" said Darren. "There's no way anyone's going to see *my* pants."

"Eugene!" pleaded Bertie. "You'll do it, won't you?"

Eugene shook his head. "Sorry, Bertie.

Dirty Bertie

I don't think my mum would let me."

Bertie slumped back in his seat and stared out the window, miserably. So much for friends. He was on his own.

Back in class, Bertie racked his brains. What was he going to do? Why oh why had he let Nick trick him into that stupid bet? He was certain that two-faced toad must have cheated. He was probably wearing half his clothes before the race even started.

In any case there was no going back now. A bet was a bet and he'd shaken on it. He tried to imagine walking into school wearing nothing but his pants. It didn't bear thinking about. People would be laughing at him for the next billion years.

Dirty Bertie

No, he'd just have to think of some way out.

BRIIIING! The bell sounded for break. Bertie trudged out to the playground, lost in thought.

"Hee hee! There he is!"

Bertie turned round to see Angela Nicely and two of her little friends. Angela lived next door to Bertie. She was six years old and had been in love with Bertie ever since the time he gave her a sherbet lemon to stop her talking.

"What do you want?" glared Bertie.

"Hee hee! We want to ... hee hee! ... ask you something!" giggled Angela.

"Not now," said Bertie. "I'm busy!" He walked faster but Angela kept up with him.

"What colour are they, Bertie?" she simpered.

"Eh?" said Bertie.

"White or pink?" giggled Laura.

"Frilly or spotty?" sniggered Yasmin.

Bertie swung round to face them. "What are you talking about?"

"Your pants!" squealed Angela. "Nicholas told us. You're coming to school in your pants tomorrow!"

The girls burst into a fresh fit of giggles.

Bertie turned a deep shade of pink. "I ... I'm not!" he stammered.

"Yes you are," said Angela. "Everybody says so."

"Listen! It's rubbish! I'm not!" said Bertie, desperately.

Angela edged closer to him, smiling sweetly. "I'm going to bring my camera, Bertie," she trilled. "I'm going to take a picture of you in your…"

Bertie didn't wait to hear any more. He turned and fled.

He hid in the cloakroom, till he was sure they had gone. This was worse than he'd ever imagined. Darren and Eugene knew. So did Angela and her friends. By now the news would be round the whole school. He should have guessed that big-mouth Nick would tell everyone. Tomorrow they'd all be waiting for him – whispering and sniggering.

Dirty Bertie

If only he could think of some way out. Bertie considered himself a master of clever plots and cunning plans, but this time his mind was blank. It was no use. He wished he was a worm so he could crawl into a hole and hide.

CHAPTER 3

"BERTIE!" boomed Miss Skinner in assembly. "Out to the front, now!"

"Me, Miss?" said Bertie.

"Yes, you. And make it snappy, I haven't got all day!"

Bertie gulped and dragged himself out to the front. Why was everyone staring at him and sniggering?

Dirty Bertie

"Haven't you forgotten something, Bertie?" said Miss Skinner.

Bertie looked down. He gasped. He was wearing nothing but his pants.

"ARGHHHHH!" he screamed – and woke up. He breathed a sigh of relief and sank back on his pillow. Thank goodness, it was only a nightmare. But wait – what was today? Friday! Pants Day! It wasn't a nightmare after all, it was really happening!

Dirty Bertie

There was a knock on the door. Mum came in. "Aren't you up yet, Bertie? It's time for school."

"Urrrhh!" groaned Bertie. "I don't feel well. I think I've got Germy Measles."

Mum felt his head. "Hmm," she said. "I can't see any spots."

"I think they're invisible!" he mumbled.

"Don't be silly, Bertie. There's no such thing."

"How do you know?" said Bertie. "If they're invisible they could be all over me! I could be dying of them! I could—"

"Get dressed!" said Mum. "You're going to school."

Bertie flopped out of bed. He pulled out his drawer and looked inside. All of his pants were teeny-weeny. What he needed was extra-large pants to cover as much of him as possible. Wait a moment – his dad had lots of pairs of pants. Big pants. Surely he could borrow a pair?

Bertie tiptoed into his parents' room. He pulled open a drawer and dumped piles of pants on to the floor. Right at the bottom he found what he was looking for. A large pair of blue Y-fronts.

Bertie tried them on and looked in the mirror. They looked absurdly big, but they were the best he could find.

Dirty Bertie

Mum and Suzy were eating breakfast in the kitchen. Bertie tried to sneak past them and reach his chair.

"HA! HA!" shrieked Suzy, catching sight of him.

"What?" said Bertie. "They're only pants."

Mum stared at him. "Good heavens, Bertie! Where are your clothes? And whose pants are those?"

"Dad's. I just need to borrow them!" said Bertie.

"Ha ha! Hee hee!" wheezed Suzy. "You should see yourself!"

"They're way too big," said Mum. "You've got plenty of pants of your own."

"Not like these. I need a really big pair!"

"Whatever for?"

"For a bet. I said I'd go to school in my
pants!"

"Don't be ridiculous, Bertie. You can't
possibly!" said Mum.

Bertie blinked. A wave of relief swept
over him. Why hadn't he thought of it
before? He had promised to go to
school in his pants and he would.

29

"Never mind!" he laughed. "It's OK. Everything's OK!"

He danced out of the kitchen and back upstairs wearing the pants on his head.

CHAPTER 4

Know-All Nick stood on the wall,
keeping watch along the street. It was
ten to nine and the playground was full
to bursting. Everyone had come early to
be sure of seeing Bertie's big moment.
Angela Nicely had her camera at the
ready. Darren, Donna and Eugene were
arguing about whether Bertie would

actually go through with it. Darren said yes. Donna said no. Eugene couldn't make up his mind.

"Here he comes!" shouted Nick, pointing up the road.

They all watched the entrance, eagerly. Bertie rounded the corner and marched in through the gates. Know-All Nick stared in disbelief. Bertie was dressed as normal in his jumper and jeans.

Nick jumped down from the wall and

Dirty Bertie

marched up to him.

"We had a bet!" he fumed. "You cheated! You had to come to school in your pants!"

Bertie shrugged. "I have. I'm wearing them. Under my trousers."

"Wh … wh … what?" stammered Nick, turning pale.

"What's the matter, Nick?" asked Bertie. "Don't *you* wear pants under your trousers?"

"Of course I do," snapped Nick.

Bertie winked at Darren. "That's not what I heard. I heard you don't wear pants."

"No," grinned Darren. "None at all."

"I do!" protested Nick.

"I heard you went knickerless. Knickerless Nick," said Bertie.

"It's not true!" wailed Nick.

"But how do we know?" said Bertie.

"Because I say so!"

"You might be lying."

"I'M NOT!" yelled Nick. "LOOK!" He pulled down his trousers to prove it.

SNAP! went Angela's camera. Nick turned crimson. The whole school could see his pants and they were all laughing.

"I'll get you for this, Bertie!" he yelled.

Dirty Bertie

FAME!

CHAPTER 1

Bertie flung open the door and
burst into the kitchen.

"I'd do anyfing for you, dear, anyfing!
'Cos you mean everyfing to meeeeee!"
he sang in his gruff, droning voice.

Suzy groaned. Dad covered his ears.

"Lovely, Bertie," said Mum. "But maybe
not quite so loud."

Dirty Bertie

"Miss Boot says you should sing out," said Bertie. "I was singing out."

"We heard you," said Dad. He glanced at his watch. "We'd better go or we'll be late for the audition."

"Good luck, Bertie," said Mum. "Just do your best. And try not to cause any trouble."

Bertie trooped out to the car. He didn't see what trouble you could cause just by singing. He had been looking forward to the audition ever since he'd heard his parents talking about it. Bertie's dad belonged to the Pudsley Players and every year the Players put on a show at the local theatre. This year they were doing the musical, *Oliver!* Bertie had seen *Oliver!* on TV. It was about an orphan called Oliver who goes round

Dirty Bertie

asking people for more and ends up rich.
When his dad said they were looking for
children to join the cast, Bertie had
jumped at the chance. He practised his
singing as they drove to the theatre.

"I'd do anyfing…" he droned.

"Bertie!" sighed Dad.

"What? I'm only singing."

"Well don't! You'll cause an accident.
And at least try to keep to the tune."

Dirty Bertie

"I am keeping to the tune!" said Bertie. "That's how it goes… 'I'd do ANYFING…!'"

"BERTIE!" shouted Dad, gripping the steering wheel.

Bertie lapsed into silence. The trouble with some people, he thought, was they just didn't appreciate good singing.

At the theatre he found the dressing room crowded with eager children waiting to be called on stage. Bertie elbowed his way through the crowd and found an empty seat next to a pale boy wearing a large brown cap. It was only when the boy looked up and scowled that he recognized his old enemy, Know-All Nick.

Dirty Bertie

"What are you doing here?" sneered Nick.

"What are *you* doing here?" replied Bertie.

"If you must know I'm going to be in the play," boasted Nick.

"Well so am I," said Bertie.

"Huh!" scoffed Nick. "They're not that desperate. Anyway, Miss Lavish only wants five boys. You don't stand a chance."

"Who's Miss Lavish?" asked Bertie.

"Don't you know? She's the director." Nick removed his cap and smoothed back his hair. "Anyway which part do you want?"

"The Artful Dodger," said Bertie.

Nick snorted. "Sorry, that part's taken. I'm going to be Dodger."

Dirty Bertie

"Liar," said Bertie. "She hasn't even heard you sing yet."

Nick gave him a smug look. "That's what you think."

A woman with a clipboard poked her head around the door.

"Nicholas?" she said. "Miss Lavish is

ready for you now."

Know-All Nick pulled on his cap and went to the door. "Oh by the way, Bertie," he said. "Miss Lavish has heard me sing lots of times. She's my godmother." He stuck out his tongue and vanished through the door.

CHAPTER 2

Bertie sat in the dressing room waiting
to be called. He would show that sneaky
slimeball, Nick. His audition would be so
good Miss Lavish would fall on her knees
and beg him to play the Artful Dodger.
The room started to empty slowly as,
one by one, the other children were
called on stage. An hour went by.

Dirty Bertie

Bertie was the only one left in the dressing room.

"Bertie?" said the lady with the clipboard. "Miss Lavish will see you now. And please don't pick your nose." Bertie removed his finger. He bet the Artful Dodger picked his nose all the time.

Bertie stood in the middle of the stage and squinted into the spotlights. He'd never been on a stage before and he'd certainly never been asked to sing a solo. Miss Lavish sat a few rows back, scribbling notes. She was a large woman wrapped in a scarlet shawl. Bertie coughed nervously. Miss Lavish looked up.

"Hello dear. And you are?"

Dirty Bertie

"Bertie," said Bertie.

"Lovely. And what are you going to sing for us?"

"Oh um … 'I'd do Anyfing'. It's from *Oliver!*" said Bertie.

Dirty Bertie

"I know where it's from, dear," said
Miss Lavish, peering over her glasses.
She raised a plump finger. "Come in with
the piano then."

Miss Plunk played the opening bars on
the piano. Bertie turned and walked off
stage.

"Where are you going now?" cried
Miss Lavish. "Come back!"

"You said to come in with the piano,"
said Bertie. "I can't come in if I'm still
here."

"I meant come in singing. Come in
with the music!"

"Oh," said Bertie. He wished she'd say
what she meant.

Miss Lavish nodded wearily at Miss
Plunk. "Let's try again, shall we?"

The piano played. Bertie took a deep

breath and opened his mouth. To his horror he realized that the words had gone clean out of his head. He had practised them a million times but his mind was a total blank. He began anyway, hoping the words would come back to him.

Dirty Bertie

"I'd um ... anyfing ... um ... you ... um ... anyfing! 'Cos you um ... anyfing! ... um er ..."

Miss Lavish's mouth had fallen open. Whatever Bertie was singing it wasn't a tune. She raised a hand to put a stop to the awful dirge, but Bertie ploughed on, bellowing any word he could remember.

Dirty Bertie

"I'd … er … ANYFING! And you'd um … ANYFING!"

"Stop!" begged Miss Lavish, waving her hands. "Stop, stop, STOP!"

Bertie stopped. He waited for Miss Lavish to start clapping. True, he had missed out one or two of the words, but no one could say he hadn't sung out. He bet no one else had sung out quite as well as he had. Miss Lavish took off her glasses.

"Thank you, Billy, that was ah … lovely. But I'm afraid I have all the children I need."

Bertie blinked. "Oh."

"But thank you so much for coming."

Bertie sniffed and wiped his nose. "You don't want me to be the Artful Dodger?" he asked.

Dirty Bertie

Miss Lavish shook her head. "No, dear, we have our Dodger already."

Know-All Nick waved to Bertie from behind the stage curtain, with a "told-you-so" smile on his face.

"I could sing something else," offered Bertie. "I know lots of songs."

"No, no more, please," said Miss Lavish hastily. "Run along now."

Bertie dug his hands in his pockets and trailed off.

Miss Lavish's assistant leaned over and whispered something in her ear.

"Wait one moment, dear!" she called. Bertie was back in an instant.

"I gather there is one very small part we have yet to cast," said Miss Lavish.

"Yes?" said Bertie.

"Well, what we really need is a dog."

Dirty Bertie

"A dog?" said Bertie.

"Yes, the costume's rather small but you look about the right size. What do you think?"

"Me?" said Bertie. "Play a dog?"

"Yes. If you wouldn't mind?"

Mind? Bertie's eyes shone. It was a dream come true!

CHAPTER 3

Mum was waiting for them when they got home.

"Well? How did it go?" she asked.

Bertie took off his coat. "Great. I got the part," he said.

"Really? They want you to be the Artful Dodger?"

"No, better than that. They want me

to be the dog," said Bertie.

"The dog?" Mum turned to Dad. "What dog?"

"It seems Mr Dodds needs a dog. He's playing Bill Sykes," explained Dad. "And they asked Bertie to do it."

"I get a costume and everything," said Bertie. "Miss Lavish says I ought to start practising right away." He padded past them on all fours and picked up Whiffer's bowl in his mouth. He dropped it at Mum's feet and began to whine.

Dirty Bertie

Mum looked at Dad. "How many weeks do we have of this?"

"Ten," sighed Dad. "Look at it this way, at least he won't be singing."

Over the next ten weeks, Bertie went to rehearsals with his dad. His part turned out to be less exciting than he had hoped. Most of the time he had to trot after Mr Dodds or sit quietly while the other actors talked on and on. His big moment came in the final act when he dashed to the front of the stage and barked to bring the police running. Bertie practised that one "Woof!" a hundred different ways, but he couldn't help feeling his talents were going to waste.

Dirty Bertie

In rehearsals he tried to add in a few "doggy touches" to liven up the dull bits of the play. Whenever Know-All Nick came on stage, Bertie bared his teeth and growled fiercely. But Miss Lavish said his growling was drowning out the words and could he please keep quiet. Bertie took to scratching his ear with his paw. But Miss Lavish said he was "destroying the atmosphere" and could he please keep still.

The following week, Bertie thought he could smell a cat and went sniffing

around the stage. Miss Lavish lost her
temper and threw down her script.
Bertie sighed. He didn't see how he was
meant to play a dog that didn't growl,
scratch or even sniff. He might as well be
a goldfish! To make matters worse, there
was still no sign of his costume. Bertie
didn't have a chance to try it on until
the dress rehearsal. It was an itchy
brown suit. The head had floppy ears
attached and was three sizes too small.
Bertie complained to Miss Lavish but she
said she didn't have time for silly details.

CHAPTER 4

Finally the big night arrived. There was a buzz of excitement as Mum and Suzy took their seats and the lights went down. The curtain drew back to reveal the painted streets of London Town.

Backstage, Bertie was still in the dressing room. "Hurry up! We're starting!" said Nick, pulling on his jacket.

Dirty Bertie

"It's this head!" moaned Bertie. "It's got smaller. I can't get it on!"

"Oh give it here!" said Nick, impatiently. He grabbed the dog's head and jammed it down hard over Bertie.

"Mmmnff!" said Bertie in a muffled voice. "That's the wrong way round! I can't see!"

Nick wasn't listening. He had hurried out of the door, anxious not to miss his cue. Bertie tried to twist the dog head back round, but it was jammed on tight and wouldn't budge.

Dirty Bertie

Mum and Suzy clapped as the first act came to an end

"Where's Bertie?" whispered Suzy. "I haven't seen him yet."

"Shhh!" replied Mum. "This is his big entrance."

Mr Dodds entered as Bill Sykes, making his way to Fagin's hideout. He looked round for his faithful dog, Bullseye, but there was no sign of him.

"Bertie!" he hissed. "Bertie!"

Backstage Dad looked round. "Where's Bertie? He should be on stage!"

At that moment, Bertie stumbled up the steps, still wrestling with his head.

"You're meant to be on," Dad hissed. He grabbed Bertie by the arm and

shoved him on stage. There were giggles
from the audience.

"What's he doing?" whispered Suzy.

"Oh dear," said Mum. "I think he's got
his head on back to front."

Mr Dodds took hold of Bullseye's
head and tried to twist it round. The
audience roared with laughter.

"Ow!" said Bertie loudly. "That hurts!"

Mr Dodds was sweating. "Shhh!" he muttered, thrusting Bertie behind a lamp-post where he couldn't do any harm. "Stay!" he commanded.

Sykes and Fagin started an argument but no one was paying much attention. They were all watching Bullseye. Bertie was rolling around on the ground, tugging at his head with both hands.

"Is this part of the story?" whispered Suzy.

"I'm not sure," replied Mum. "I don't remember it in the film."

Watching from the wings, Miss Lavish ground her teeth. At this rate Bertie would ruin everything!

"Miss Plunk!" she hissed. "Miss Plunk! Start the next song."

Dirty Bertie

Miss Plunk thumped on the piano. Fagin sang "You've got to pick a pocket or two" and Dodger and his gang began to dance.

"Bertie! Get off!" urged Dad. Bertie trotted blindly in the wrong direction – straight towards the dancers who were whirling faster and faster.

Know-All Nick took a step back, tripped over Bertie, and tumbled straight into an apple cart. Apples spilled across the stage and under the dancers' feet. Miss Lavish watched in horror as Mr Dodds stumbled into a lamp-post and sent it crashing down on the streets of London. The tall scenery swayed dangerously.

"Look out!" shouted Dad. "It's going to fall!"

Dirty Bertie

"Arghhhh!" screamed the actors, running in all directions.

"What's happening?" asked Bertie, left alone on stage.

CRASH! went the scenery as it came tumbling down.

There was a hushed silence. The audience waited to see if this was the end of the show. Slowly the dust cleared to reveal a mound of broken scenery.

Dirty Bertie

A door moved. From underneath it,
Bertie scrambled out. He tugged at his
dog's head and finally managed to pull it
off. Puzzled, he looked around. *Where
had everybody gone?* The audience were
all staring at him in astonishment. Bertie
suddenly remembered he hadn't given
his one and only line.

Dirty Bertie

"WOOF!" he barked.

The audience laughed and clapped and cheered. Bertie grinned and gave a low bow. He was still bowing when Dad brought the curtain down.

Dirty Bertie

Turning round, he saw Miss Lavish, Mr Dodds and the rest of the cast advancing on him. Their hair was white with dust and their faces were grim.

"You wait," said Miss Lavish. "You just wait…"

But Bertie didn't wait. He did what any dog would do – he took to his heels and ran.

AVAST THERE ME HEARTIES!
Come to Black-Eyed
Bertie's Pirate Party
Saturday 2 pm
Dress as a pirate
P.S. ~ Bring me a Present or
Walk ye Plank!

CHAPTER 1

Bertie could hardly wait — he'd been
counting down the days to his birthday
for weeks and now it was almost here.
It was going to be the best party ever.
Bertie already had his pirate captain's
hat and plastic eyepatch. All he had
to do now was hand out invitations to
his friends.

Dirty Bertie

"A pirate party? Great!" said Darren. "When is it?"

"Saturday afternoon," said Bertie.

"Not this Saturday?"

"Yes!"

Darren's face fell. "But I'm going to Royston's party!"

"Royston's?" Bertie couldn't believe his ears. Royston Rich was the biggest show-off in the school and no one in Bertie's class liked him. "But you hate Royston!"

Dirty Bertie

"I know but he's having a swimming party. He's got a pool in his garden with a wave machine and everything!"

"But what about my party?"

Darren shrugged. "Sorry, Bertie. Royston gave out his invitations last week. Didn't you get one?"

Bertie hadn't. Not that he cared. Who wanted to go to Royston's rubbish party? He crossed Darren's name off his list. Still, if Darren let him down at least he could rely on Eugene…

"Saturday?" asked Eugene.

"Yes. You're coming, aren't you?"

Eugene turned pink. "I'd like to but I'm going to Royston's party."

"Not you as well!"

"Sorry, Bertie. He's got his own swimming pool with a—"

Dirty Bertie

"I know! A wave machine and everything!" scowled Bertie.

"Yes and did he tell you about the inflatables? It's going to be brilliant. Everyone's going…" Eugene went pinker still. "Oh – aren't you, Bertie?"

"No!" snapped Bertie. "I'm having my own party and it'll be a billion times better than his."

Scratch! Bertie crossed Eugene off his list. At break-time he gave Donna her invitation. Scratch! She was going to Royston's party too. So were Alex, Dan, Stan, Sunil and Pamela. At the end of the day the only invitation left was for Angela Nicely. Bertie hadn't wanted to invite her in the first place – he'd only included Angela because he'd gone to her party. Scratch! Out went Angela.

Dirty Bertie

That left — Bertie looked at his list — no one at all. *Well, see if I care*, thought Bertie. *I'll have a great party on my own. Loads more cake and crisps for me!* Hang on though, if no one came to his party he wouldn't get any presents. And playing pirates wasn't much fun when the only enemy was Whiffer.

CHAPTER 2

Bertie slammed the front door. He flung down his bag and clumped upstairs to his room. A minute later, Mum poked her head round the door.

"Bertie, are you all right? How was school today?"

"Terrible," grumbled Bertie. "No one's coming to my party."

Dirty Bertie

"No one? Didn't you give out the invitations?"

Bertie explained about Royston Rich's swimming party.

"Oh dear!" said Mum. "Fancy it being on the same day as yours! Maybe we should move your party to next weekend?"

"That's years away!" moaned Bertie. "If anyone should move I don't see why it should be me. Why doesn't he move his smelly old party?"

His mum sighed. "Bertie, things don't always work out the way you want."

"Huh!" said Bertie, bitterly. "I bet if we had a swimming pool everyone would come to my party. Why can't we get a swimming pool in *our* garden?"

His mum gave him one of her looks and closed the door.

Bertie lay on his bed. It wasn't fair. Who did Royston think he was pinching all Bertie's friends? Just because he didn't have any friends of his own! Well Black-Eyed Bertie, the scourge of the seven seas, wasn't beaten yet. If Royston was boasting about his super swimming pool, he would just have to think of something better. He racked his brains. What did pirates do when they weren't swabbing

decks or splicing the mainbrace?
Of course — they hunted for buried
treasure!

Bertie tiptoed into his parents' room.
He went straight to the present drawer
where his mum kept anything she didn't
want him to see. Inside he found party
hats, balloons — and a big bag of
chocolate coins. "Ahaar!" cried Bertie.
"Gold doubloons!"

Out in the garden he dug a hole and carefully slipped in the bag of coins. He was just smoothing over the earth when he heard a ring at the door.

It was Royston Rich.

"Oh hello, Bertie," said Royston, carelessly. "I brought your invitation."

Bertie stared in surprise. "You're inviting me?"

Royston shrugged. "Andrew can't come so I suppose you might as well. I couldn't think of anyone else."

"Well I can't come either, I'm having my own party," said Bertie.

"I know, but no one's going to yours, are they?" gloated Royston.

"Huh, that's what you think! Loads of people are coming."

"Yeah? Like who?"

"Like … loads of people."

"Well everyone from our class is going to be at *my* party," boasted Royston. He pushed the invitation under Bertie's nose. "Keep it anyway, in case you change your mind."

Bertie snatched it off him. "I won't," he said.

"Suit yourself," said Royston. "You'll be missing the best party of the year. We're having a wave…"

Dirty Bertie

SLAM! Bertie shut the door in his face.

He turned round to find Mum barring his way.

"Bertie, someone's been nosing in the present drawer."

"Oh. Have they?" said Bertie, innocently.

"Yes and a bag of chocolate coins is missing. I bought them as prizes for your party. Do you know anything about that?"

Dirty Bertie

"Erm…" said Bertie.

"Bertie, if I find out you've eaten them…"

"I haven't!"

"Good, then you can give them back. Right now."

"But Mum, I need them for the treasure hunt! You can't have a pirate party without buried treasure."

Mum put a hand to her head. "Buried treasure? Bertie you haven't!"

"What?"

"Buried them?"

"Well I might have," said Bertie. "But it's OK, I know exactly where they are!"

"Where?" demanded Mum.

"Um … somewhere in the garden."

CHAPTER 3

Saturday afternoon came. Bertie stood at the front room window staring along the road. He was dressed in his pirate hat and eyepatch. Whiffer, his faithful sea dog, sat at his side keeping watch.
It was half past two.

His mum came and joined him at the window. "I'm sorry, Bertie, I don't think

Dirty Bertie

anyone's coming. Why don't you go to Royston's party? It's not too late."

"I don't want to!" glared Bertie.

"I'm sure you'll have fun," said Mum.

"I won't. I hate swimming!"

"Don't be silly, Bertie. All your friends will be there."

"Huh!" scowled Bertie. "I haven't got any friends."

Mum sighed. "Look, we'll have your party another day. Why don't you just go and enjoy yourself?"

"All right, all right!" said Bertie. "As long as Whiffer can come too."

Mum frowned. "It's a swimming party, Bertie, dogs aren't invited."

"Then I'm not going," said Bertie stubbornly. "If Whiffer can't go then I'm not going either."

Dirty Bertie

Ten minutes later they arrived at Royston's big house on Poshley Drive. Bertie's mum buzzed the intercom at the gates.

"Do come through!" sang Mrs Rich's voice. "We're in the pool!"

The gates swung slowly open and Bertie trudged through with Whiffer at his heels. Screams and laughter came from the enormous swimming pool in the back garden.

"Hi Bertie!" waved Darren, zooming down the slide and landing with a splash.

Royston looked up. "Oh hello, Bertie! I thought you were too busy to come?"

Dirty Bertie

Dirty Bertie

"I can't stay long," said Bertie, looking at his watch. "I've got people waiting."

"What do you think of my swimming pool? Super isn't it?"

Bertie shrugged. "It's all right."

"You better get changed. We're just about to start the wave machine!"

Bertie wandered over to the barbecue where Mr Rich was cooking hot dogs and enormous steaks. Whiffer's nose twitched at the smell of sausages.

"Hey!" shouted Mr Rich.

Bertie looked up. "Me?"

"Yes, you. Is that your dog?"

Bertie glanced down at Whiffer who was sniffing the meat. "He likes sausages."

"I don't care what he likes, take him somewhere else and tie him up. I don't want him near the food!"

Dirty Bertie

Bertie dragged Whiffer away and tied him to a post on the lawn tennis court. "Sorry, Whiffer," said Bertie. "You stay there and I'll get you something to eat!"

Whiffer whined and pulled at his lead.

"Sit!" commanded Bertie. "Sit!" Whiffer sniffed around then squatted down on his hind legs. Uh-oh — that could only mean one thing. Bertie glanced around, hoping no one had noticed. It was lucky he'd remembered to bring along his pooper-scooper just in case. He scooped the lump of poop into a small plastic bag. Now where to get rid of it?

Dirty Bertie

He wandered back to the house,
holding the bag at arm's length. By the
pool he almost bumped into Mrs Rich
carrying a tray of lemonade. Mrs Rich
stopped and stared at the bag in Bertie's
hand. She looked closer. Was that…?
Good heavens! It was! She gasped.

"It's all right, it's only dog poo," said
Bertie, holding the bag up for inspection.

Dirty Bertie

"Ugh! Take it away!" cried Mrs Rich.

"I am taking it away," said Bertie. "But I'm looking for a bin."

"By the back door!" Mrs Rich flapped a hand. "Take it away before you drop it!"

Bertie walked on. He didn't see why Royston's mum was making such a big fuss. After all, dogs had to poo just like everyone else. And he'd been to a lot of trouble clearing it up – you would have thought she'd be grateful!

He was so busy grumbling to himself that he didn't notice the paper plate of raspberry jelly lying right in his path. Bertie stepped in the jelly and slipped. "Woaaaaaahhh!" He lost his balance and the bag slipped from his grasp. It sailed into the air and the lump of poop shot out like a torpedo.

Dirty Bertie

Up, up, up it rose…

Then down, down, down – landing in the swimming pool with a loud PLOP!

"Uh-oh," said Bertie.

CHAPTER 4

Royston zoomed down the slide, landing in the deep end with a great splash. He came up spluttering for air. What was that floating in the water? Something brown like a leaf.

"ARGGHHHH!" he shrieked. "A POO! THERE'S A POO IN THE POOL!"

Bertie had never dreamed one little piece of doggy-do could cause so much panic. Thirty children scrambled to get out of the pool, screaming as if a killer shark was after them.

"Do something!" cried Mrs Rich to her husband.

Mr Rich fetched a net and fished around in the deep end. But the poop had sunk to

the bottom and didn't want to be caught.

"Don't worry," said Royston. "My dad'll sort it out. Then we can all go back in."

"Eeugh!" Donna pulled a face. "I'm not going in there!"

"Nor me," said Pamela. "It's full of pooey germs."

"It's yucky!"

"It's smelly!"

"But what about the party?" asked Eugene. "What are we going to do?"

Bertie pulled on his eyepatch and leaped on to a sunbed.

"Who wants to come back to my house for a pirate party?" he cried.

"Can we have sword fights?" asked Darren.

"Of course!" nodded Bertie. "And walking the plank. And a treasure hunt — with real chocolate coins!"

Dirty Bertie

"Chocolate? Why didn't you say so before?" said Darren. "Come on!"

Thirty children charged out of the gates and down the road with Black-Eyed Bertie leading the way. It was going to be a brilliant birthday after all, he thought, and all thanks to Whiffer and his pongy present!

Out now: